Once
upon
a breath

Oh, EXCUSE ME, I WAS JUST PRACTICING MY SAX.
Let ME INTRODUCE MYSELF - MY NAME IS B.B. WOLF
THEY CALL ME B.B. CUZ I'M
BIG
AND I'M
BAD!

THIS HERE IS MY VERY fine ESTABLISHMENT, THE BIG BAD WOLF BLUES CLUB.

I PERFORM HERE WITH MY BAND -THE *little pigs three*- FOR ALL OF MY FANS.

I'LL TELL YOU SOMETHING ELSE ABOUT MYSELF. I'VE GOT ASTHMA. YOU'RE THINKING "A *famous*, BIG, BAD, JAZZ LOV'IN, *sax play'in* WOLF LIKE YOU?" *That's right.* I'VE HAD IT SINCE I WAS A <u>NOT</u> SO BIG <u>NOT</u> SO BAD WOLF.

BUT I DON'T LET ASTHMA GIVE ME THE *blues.* I JUST MAKE SURE TO TAKE MY MEDICINE AND TRY TO AVOID THE THINGS THAT CAN TRIGGER MY ASTHMA. I HAVE LEARNED TO SPOT MY *triggers* AND STAY COOL.

But it wasn't always this easy.

I REMEMBER ONE DAY WHEN I WAS
JUST STARTING OUT...
I WOKE UP THAT
MORNING,
CHECKED
MYSELF
OUT IN
THE
MIRROR
-beautiful-

-AND TOOK MY DAILY MEDICATION.

I ALWAYS USE A preventor puffer TO START MY DAY.

I thought I better clean up my place. I vacuumed to get rid of dust mites in the carpet and bedding. I'm allergic to them and they can act as one of my triggers.

But, FOR SOME REASON, my vacuum WOULDN'T WORK.

I FIGURED I BETTER GET IT checked out.

SMALL APPLIANCE REPAIR Shop
JUST as I WAS COMING OUT OF THE SMALL APPLIANCE repair shop...

a BEATEN OLD JALOPY
—with 3 little pigs inside—
DROVE BY SPEWING DANGEROUS
FUMES FROM ITS BROKEN
eXHAUST.

I chased AFTER THEM TO EXPLAIN HOW air pollution IS BAD FOR EVERYONE BUT ESPECIALLY FOR THOSE WITH asthma.

"NOT BY THE HAIR OF YOUR CHINNY CHIN CHIN," THEY CALLED BACK.
"Then I'll HUFF and I'll PUFF and..."

Just THEN the LIGHT turned GREEN and THEY SPED OFF.

DARN PIGS!

ANYWAY, I HAD TO GET OVER TO THE PARK FOR MY BASKETBALL GAME DURING THE GAME I NOTICED THAT MY ALLERGIES WERE BOTHERING ME.

THERE SURE WAS A LOT OF RAGWEED POLLEN IN THE AIR.

I TURNED TO SEE IT WAS THOSE *pesky pigs* AGAIN.

JUST AS I WAS ABOUT TO GO AFTER THEM SOMEONE PASSED ME THE BALL.
Those pigs GOT AWAY, but I SCORED THE winning basket.

IT WAS GETTING LATE AND I HAD TO GET TO

No cats allowed

WHEN I GOT THERE MY CHEST FELT TIGHT AND I BEGAN TO COUGH. DARN RAGWEED.

I USED MY RELIEVER PUFFER TO HELP ME FEEL BETTER. I WANTED TO BE IN GOOD SHAPE FOR MY SHOW. THAT NIGHT, SOME TROUBLE STARTED. MY CLUB HAS ONE IMPORTANT RULE.

"no cats allowed!"

hey, I DIG CATS BUT I'M ALLERGIC TO THEM. AND WOULDN'T YOU KNOW, THERE WERE THOSE DEVIOUS PIGS SNEAKING THEIR PET CATS INTO MY CLUB.
I RAN OVER TO SAY "hey man THIS ISN'T COOL, WE'VE GOT A NO CATS RULE,"

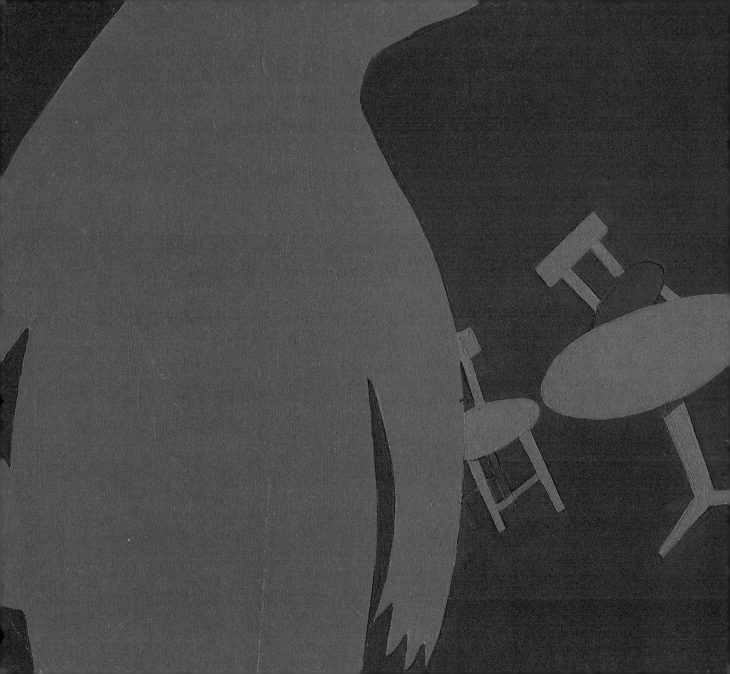

"YO, LITTLE PIGS, LITTLE PIGS, LET ME IN,"
I yelled, BANGING ON THE DOOR.
"NOT BY THE HAIR OF YOUR CHINNY CHIN CHIN,"
they cried BACK.

"then I'll HUFF and I'll PUFF and..."

JUST then I HEARD THE announcement FROM THE OTHER ROOM.

So I had to go on STAGE.

EXIT

IN the MIDDLE OF the FIRST SET, I SAW THEM creep out.

3PIGS

3
PIGS
LIVE
here

WHEN THE
SHOW
ENDED

I KNEW I HAD A JOB
TO DO. I HAD
TO TRACK DOWN
THOSE PIGS AND
EXPLAIN ASTHMA
TO THEM.

I SPENT HOURS WALKING THE STREET BUT THEY WERE NOWHERE TO BE FOUND. JUST WHEN I WAS ABOUT TO GIVE UP, I TURNED THE CORNER AND SAW THEIR PAD. IT WOULD HAVE BEEN EASY TO MISS — WEDGED LIKE IT WAS BETWEEN THOSE TWO BIG APARTMENT BUILDINGS. I WENT UP TO THE WINDOW AND PEEKED IN ...

...there they were. THE THREE OF THEM. JUST jamming. Strumming THEIR GUITARS AND banging THEIR bongos. I KNEW EXACTLY WHAT I HAD TO DO.

"LITTLE PIGS, LITTLE PIGS, LET ME IN." I YELLED

"NOT by the HAIR OF YOUR CHINNY, CHIN CHIN," THEY YELLED BACK.

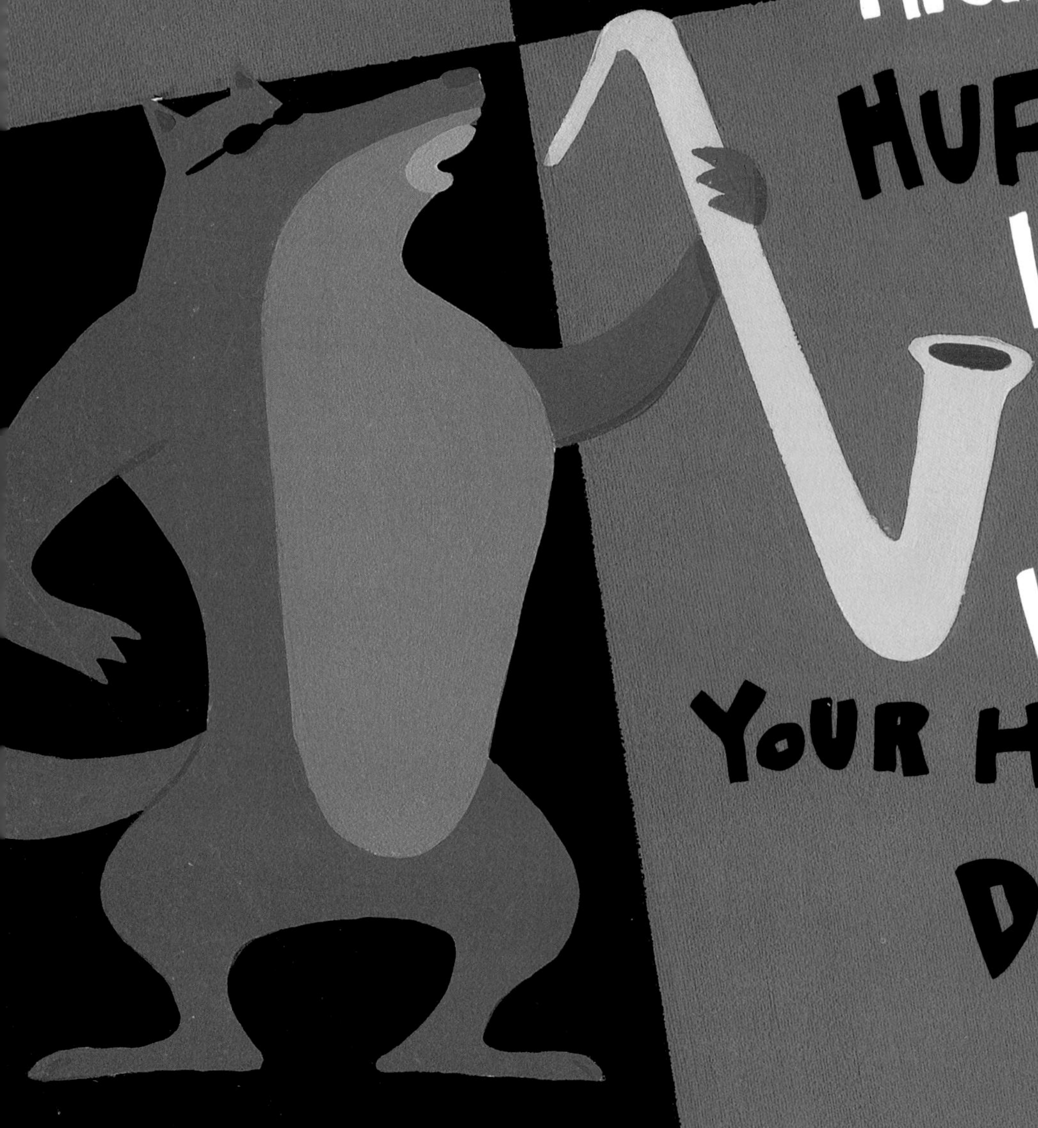

"then I'll HUFF AND I'll PUFF, and I'll BLOW YOUR HOUSE DOWN!"

...well YOU KNOW WHAT I DID.

Every NIGHT BEFORE GOING TO BED,
I WRITE IN MY ASTHMA diary.
THAT night, I HAD AN
EXTRA ENTRY.

P.S. I hired 3 new members for the band today. They are living in the spare bedroom until we rebuild their house.